THE
SECRET OF THE
SACHEM'S TREE

OTHER YEARLING BOOKS YOU WILL ENJOY:

The Little Broomstick, MARY STEWART

Good Luck Arizona Man, REX BENEDICT

The Cricket Winter, FELICE HOLMAN

Winnie-the-Pooh, A. A. MILNE

The Pooh Cook Book, VIRGINIA H. ELLISON

The Pooh Party Book, VIRGINIA H. ELLISON

The Great Cheese Conspiracy, JEAN VAN LEEUWEN

Hugo, MARIA GRIPE

Josephine, MARIA GRIPE

A Wrinkle in Time, MADELEINE L'ENGLE

YEARLING BOOKS are designed especially to entertain and enlighten young people. The finest available books for children have been selected under the direction of Dr. Charles F. Reasoner, Professor of Elementary Education, New York University; and Dr. M. Jerry Weiss, Distinguished Professor of Communications, Jersey City State College.

For a complete listing of all Yearling titles write to Education Sales Department, Dell Publishing Co., Inc., 1 Dag Hammarskjold Plaza, New York, N.Y. 10017.

About the Book

Many plans are brewing the Halloween of 1687 in Hartford, Connecticut. Two of the Wadsworth children, Hannah and Jonathan, have carved a devilish pumpkin and hidden it in the hollow of the Sachem's Tree. After dark, they plan to use it to scare Goody Gifford—for they think she's a witch.

Sir Edmund Andros is coming, on behalf of the new English king, to take away the Connecticut Charter, which has given the colony a considerable amount of self-government. And Captain Wadsworth, the children's father, plans to stop him!

How Captain Wadsworth manages to outwit Sir Edmund makes a dramatically absorbing story of unusual interest to advanced beginning readers.

F. N. Monjo, a distinguished author of historical fiction, has chosen one of Connecticut's most cherished legends as the basis for this intriguing tale. The story is further enhanced by Margot Tomes' gifted style of illustration.

ILLUSTRATED BY

MARGOT TOMES

F.N. MONJO

THE

SECRET
OF THE
SACHEM'S
TREE

A YEARLING BOOK

Published by
DELL PUBLISHING CO., INC.
1 Dag Hammarskjold Plaza
New York, N.Y. 10017

Yearling ® TM 913705, Dell Publishing Co., Inc.
Reprinted by arrangement with Coward, McCann
& Geoghegan, Inc.

Printed in the United States of America
First Yearling printing—October 1973

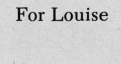

For Louise

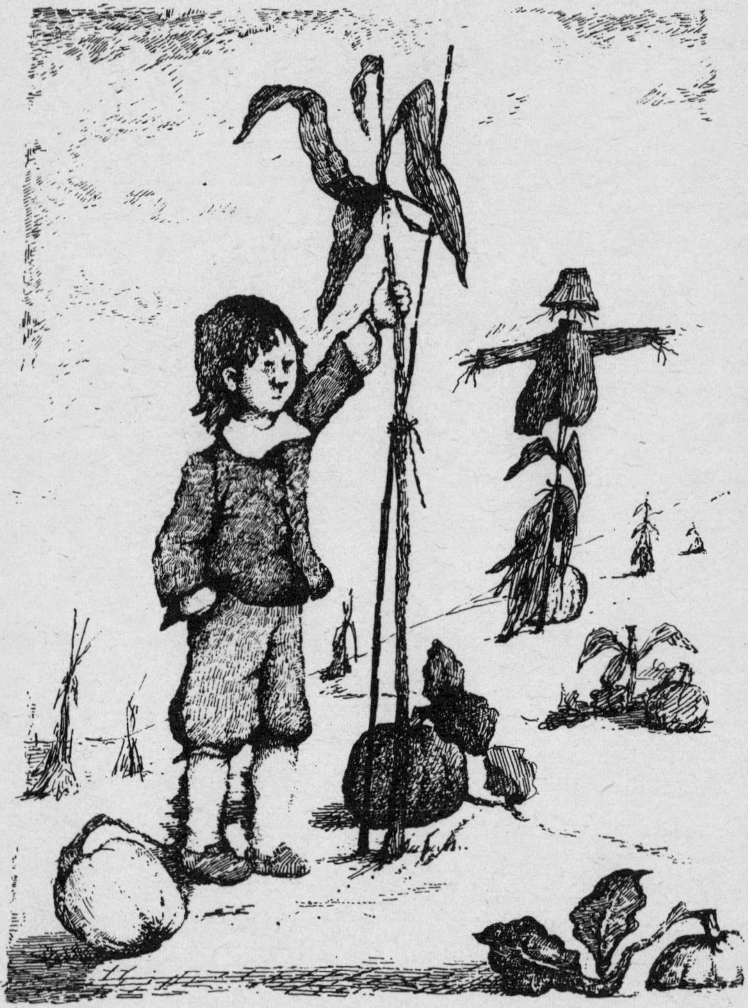

Chapter One
GOODY GIFFORD

Jonathan Wadsworth
went into his father's cornfield.
His sister Hannah went with him.
They were looking for a nice fat pumpkin.
Today was October 30,
and tomorrow would be Halloween.

All the corn had been
gathered into the barn, weeks ago.
But here and there,
in the nearly empty fields,
there were still
a few big orange pumpkins.

"There's a nice one," said Hannah.
"Aye," said Jonathan Wadsworth.
"It should do."
He broke the pumpkin
from the dry brown vine.
"And now we must show it
to Hezekiah and to Roger.
And then we must hide it somewhere
for Halloween."

Hannah and Jonathan
carried the big, round pumpkin
between them.
They crossed the frosty cornfield
and started into the woods.
Before they had gone far,
they crossed the stream
that ran past Goody Gifford's cottage.
Smoke was coming from the chimney.

"Do you believe that Goody Gifford
really is a witch?" said Hannah.
"Hezekiah says she is," said Jonathan.
"But Ichabod and Joseph
say she is not," said Hannah.
"They say that Goody Gifford
is naught but a crazed old woman.
They say she lives there,
quite at peace,
she and her cat and her cow,
doing harm to nobody."
"Besides," said Jonathan,
"Father says she *can't* be a witch,
because there are no witches at all.
Not in the whole wide world."

Hannah and Jonathan had heard
all the stories about Goody Gifford.
When a calf was born blind, people said
Goody Gifford had laid a spell on it.

When the cream in the churn went sour,
before it turned to butter, women said
that Goody Gifford had soured it,
by witchcraft!

And when the winter wind
screamed in the trees,
people said it was Goody Gifford,
crying out, for King Philip's head!

Jonathan and Hannah
looked over their shoulders
until Goody Gifford's cottage
had disappeared from sight.
The two children
were glad to leave that place
far behind them.

For sometimes Goody Gifford
and her cat, Mehitabel,
rushed out of the little cottage.
"Away! Away!" the old woman would cry.
"Leave us be!
If it had not been for King Philip's head,
I were not a widow today!"

King Philip had been an Indian Chief.
The Indians had called him their sachem.
Ten years ago, in the Indian war,
Goody Gifford's husband, Will,
had marched off with the army
to fight King Philip.
The men of Connecticut
had fought King Philip and his Indians.

They fought until the war was won.
Will had helped catch and
kill King Philip.
But Will had been killed, too,
right there in the swamp
where they killed King Philip.

When the soldiers saw the sachem dead,
they cut off King Philip's head.
They sent it to Plymouth
and nailed it up on a post
at the top of Fort Hill.

But Goody Gifford
was wild with grief.
Wild with grief
for her husband, Will.
For he never came home.
And now she and her cat, Mehitabel,
would go out into the woods, at night.
Goody Gifford would call,
"King Philip! King Philip!
Here is your head!
I'll give you back your head, King Philip,
if you give me back my Will!"
And that was why
all the people of Hartford
said that Goody Gifford was crazy.
And that was why
they called her a witch.
And that was why
they said Goody Gifford
blinded the calves,
and soured the cream,
and danced with the devil
on Halloween!

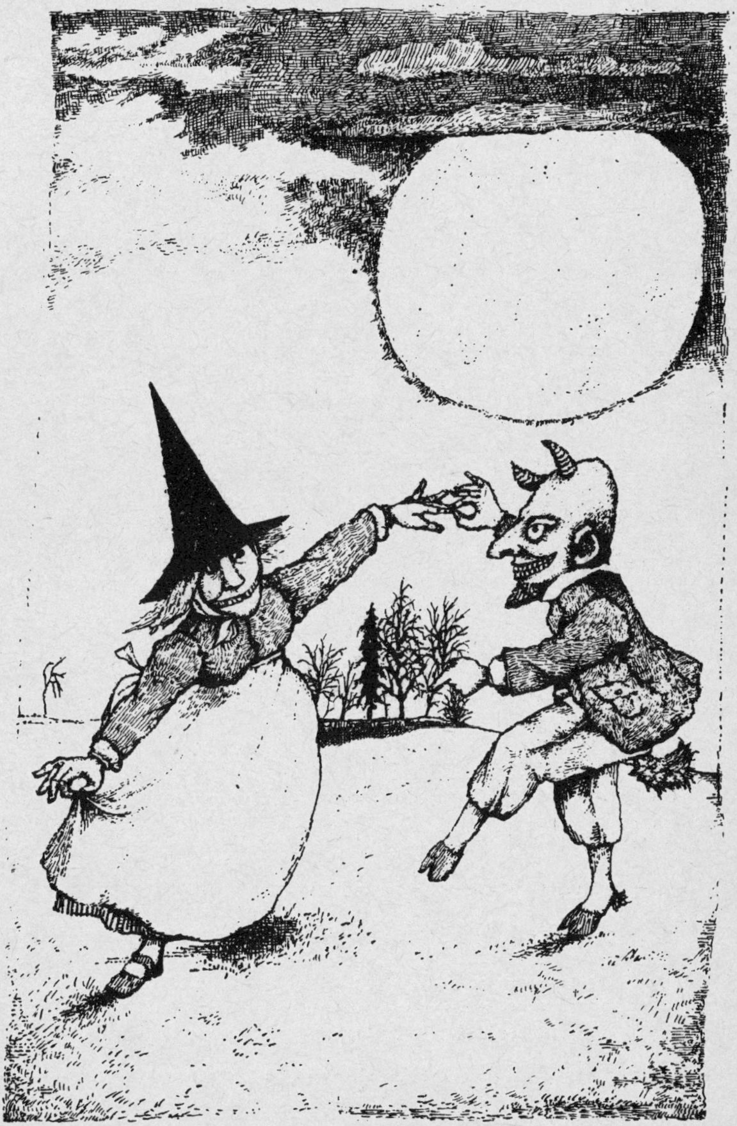

Chapter Two
THE SACHEM'S TREE

Hezekiah Wyllys took up his knife.
He had just begun carving the pumpkin.
"When Goody Gifford sees this face
we're cutting," said Hezekiah,
"she'll think it's King Philip's head, maybe.
Or maybe the head of her friend, the devil.
And she'll jump right onto her broom,
she will, and fly up over the moon!"

Jonathan Wadsworth
and his sister Hannah
and Roger Wolcott
and Hezekiah Wyllys
took two carrots and poked them
into the holes they cut in the pumpkin.
The carrots would give the devil
a pair of horns.
And they cut out eyes,
and a mouth, with teeth,
and a horrible nose,
and a beard of corn shucks.

When they were finished,
they had a terrible devil's face,
ready to frighten Goody Gifford.
Then Hezekiah said,
"Now we must hide it, somewhere safe.
We can put it in the hollow oak
that grows by my house
at the foot of the hill.
It will be safe there, until tomorrow."
"Till tomorrow night,"
said Jonathan Wadsworth.
"Tomorrow night, when it's Halloween!"

Then Hezekiah told them
the story of the oak—
the tree they called the Sachem's Tree.
For years before, when the English folk
first came to Hartford,
they had bought their land
from an Indian chief,
the sachem Sequassen.
And Sequassen had told the men of Hartford
that this was the oak, the sacred tree,
where the Indians gathered
to hold their councils.

This was the tree,
said the sachem Sequassen,
that told the tribe
when to plant its corn.
For every spring
when the buds of the oak
grew as large as the ears
of a little gray squirrel,
the Indians knew it was time to plant.
And kernels of corn
were put in the ground.

It was almost dark
when Hezekiah had finished his story.
The night wind rustled
the dry brown leaves
of the old oak tree.

Hezekiah and Hannah
and Roger and Jonathan
shivered as they hid their pumpkin
down in the hollow of the Sachem's Tree.
And all of them
were thinking of cats and witches
and the trick they would play
on Goody Gifford,
tomorrow night
on Halloween.

Chapter Three
THE SCRATCH OF A BEAR'S PAW

That night at supper
Mr. Jonathan Wadsworth
looked at his children.
He said grace to God,
asking Him to bless the food.
And his wife, Elizabeth,
began to serve the dinner.
Father Wadsworth
looked at all of them, eating—
Mother and Joseph and Ichabod

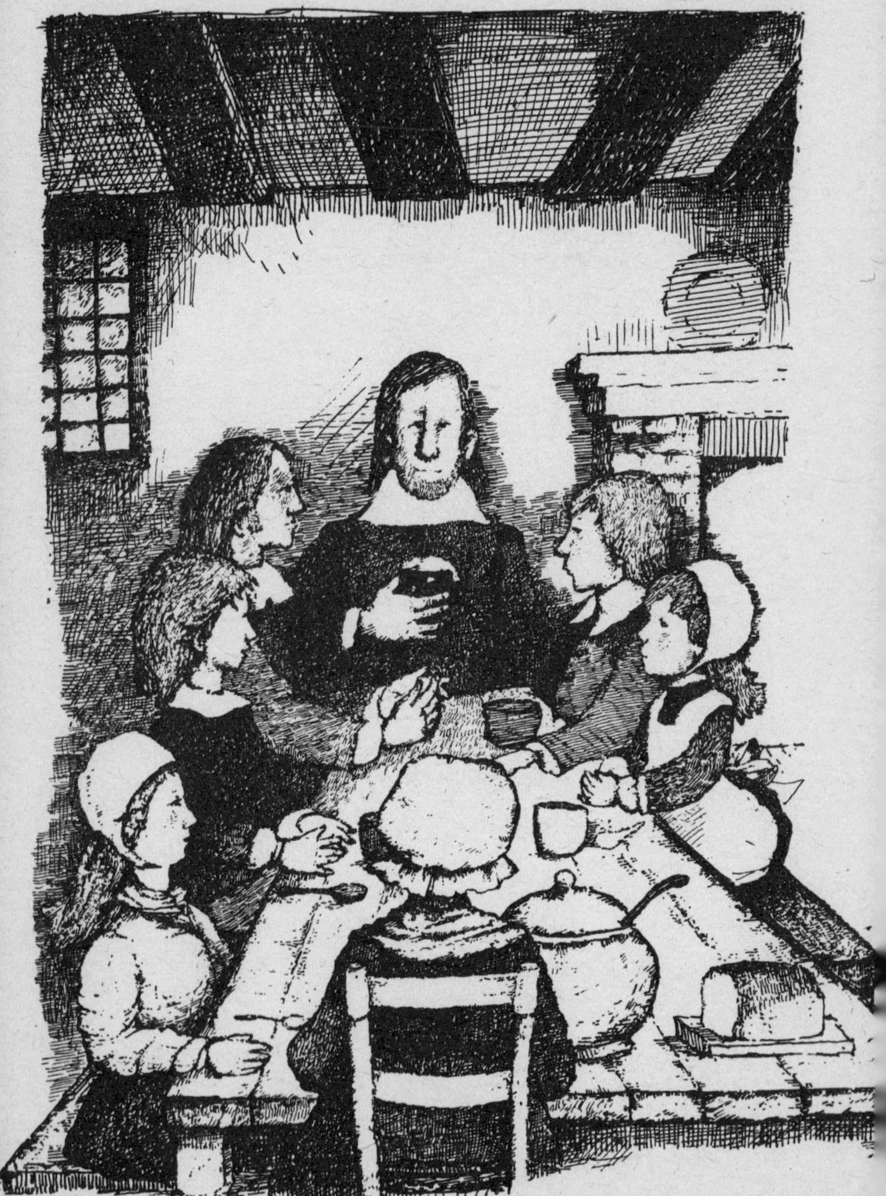

and Hannah and Liza and Jonathan—
and he drank a sip of his beer.
"Hannah and Jonathan,"
said their father,
"I saw you down by the Sachem's Tree.
Saw you there with Roger Wolcott,
and Hezekiah, the Wyllys' boy,
tucking a pumpkin into the tree.
A jack-o'-lantern, it seemed to be. . . ."
"With a devil's face cut out,
to frighten Goody Gifford,
because she's a witch!" said Jonathan.
"Yes," said Hannah.
"A witch!
And we'd like to frighten a wicked witch
on Halloween, please, Father."

"Now, Hannah," said Father, "and Jonathan,
we're plain Connecticut Puritan folk.
No dancing on May Day.
No feasting on Christmas.
Nor do we cut the devil's face
in pumpkins,
for jack-o'-lanterns, on Halloween."

"But Father—"
"No, Jonathan," said Father.
"We'll cut no pumpkins on Halloween.
Besides, Goody Gifford
is just a poor old woman
who had her husband killed
in King Philip's War—
same as we had some Wadsworths killed.
So I'll not have you call
Goody Gifford a witch!
She's only a poor old woman,
half crazy with grief,"
and Father drank some more of his beer.

JAMES II

"Besides," said Father,
"there's something far more
important than Halloween
that's happening here tomorrow."
"What is it, Father?" said Jonathan.
"All because of the king," said Father.
"The king, in London.

"That's what it's about.
After all the time we've struggled here,
to build our homes in the wild!
Now the king is sending his soldiers
to tell us the trees I've cut,
and the stones I've hauled,
and the fields I've cleared
ain't mine!" said Father.

"We bought our land, in Hartford, here,
from the Indian sachem Sequassen.
And the old King of England—
old King Charles—
said we'd bought it fair
when he sent us out our charter."
"Our charter, Father?" said Ichabod,
eating his Indian pudding.

"Yes," said Father. "Our charter.
A paper, it is, signed by old King Charles.
A paper that says Connecticut Colony
is free to make its own laws to live by.
Free to have its own courts and judges.
Aye, that charter says we're all of us free.
Free to own our lands
and to farm our farms."
"Then why would he want
to take it all back again?" said Hannah,
cutting the apple pie.
"Another king is on the throne.
King James the Second," said Father.
His face grew red and angry.
"King James is sending his man,
Sir Edmund, to take away our charter!
To take away our fields and lands,
our house and all our living.
Sir Edmund Andros comes tomorrow,
tomorrow on Halloween,
to take away our living.
The land I bought of the Indians—
of the Indian chief, Sequassen."

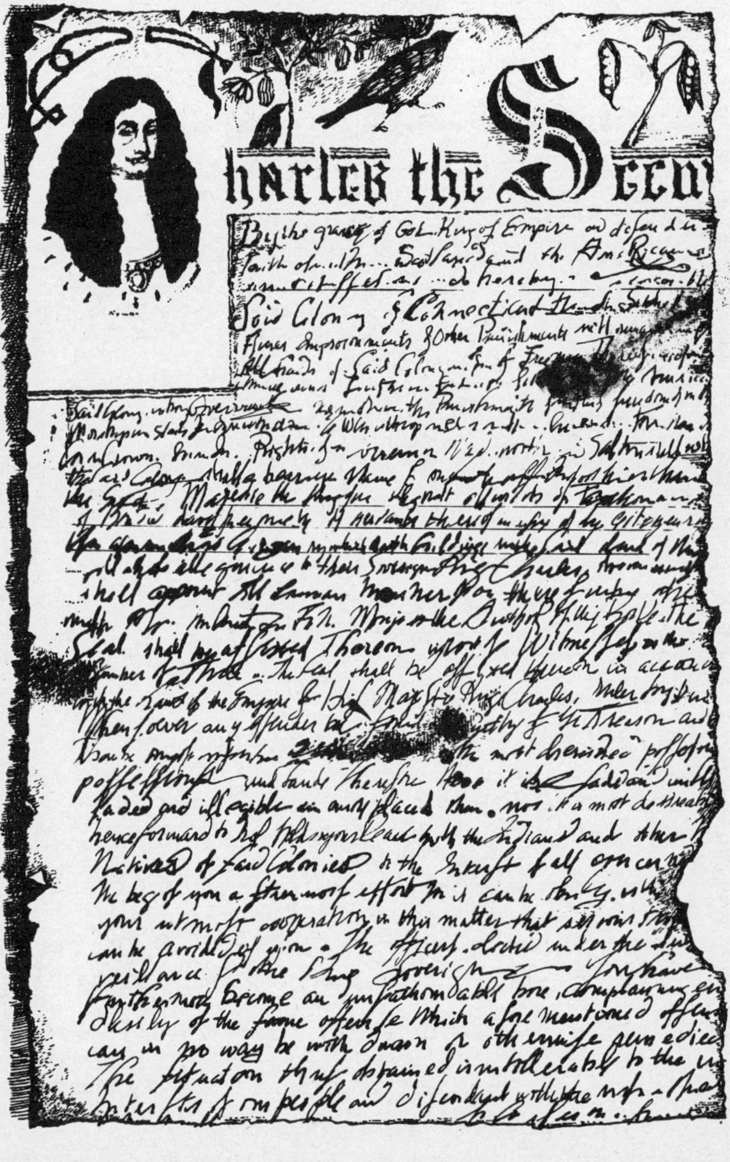
harles the Secon
By the grace of God King of Empire and defender
Said Colony of Connecticut
Fines Imprisonments & other Punishments
Whensoever any offender
faded and illegible in many places
henceforward
Natives of said Colonies
your utmost cooperation in this matter
The situation thus obtained is intolerable to the
interests of our people

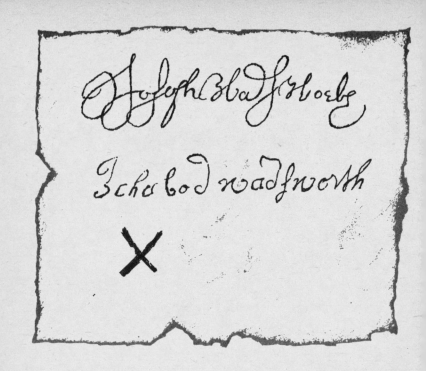

"Sequassen the sachem, who made his mark
with an *X*, like that, when we bought it!
Sir Edmund says
Sequassen's *X* is worthless!"
thundered Father.
"Sir Edmund says
an Indian's mark means *nothing!*"
thumped out Father.
"Says your fine Sir Edmund:
'The mark of an Indian means no more
than the scratch of a bear's paw!'"

"Then we must find a way," said Mother,
"to trick our fine Sir Edmund,
and keep our charter from him!"
"Aye," said Father, "we *mean* to keep it!
But *how* shall we do it?
That is the thing.
It's a dangerous matter
to anger the king.
Unless the charter were . . ."
and then Father smiled
and sipped a sip of his beer.

"Children," he said, "get rid of
that pumpkin.
And leave Goody Gifford be.
And tomorrow night, on Halloween,
Stay away from the Sachem's Tree!"

Chapter Four
THE CANDLES IN THE MEETINGHOUSE

Next morning Hannah and Jonathan
had to tell Roger Wolcott
and Hezekiah Wyllys
everything Father had ordered them to do.
The four children
went to the hollow in the Sachem's Tree
and took out the pumpkin.
They threw it away in the woods.

The children covered it
with dry brown leaves.

As it disappeared,
Jonathan kept wondering
about Sir Edmund and the charter.

Everyone else in the village
was wondering about them, too.

Late in the afternoon they heard
that Sir Edmund had crossed the river
at Wethersfield.
He and his soldiers were on their way.

On their way, to Hartford.
He was coming with judges and gentlemen.
He had two trumpeters out in front,
and twenty soldiers dressed in red
tramping along behind.
Sir Edmund was wearing
a long curly wig
and a hat with a curly plume.

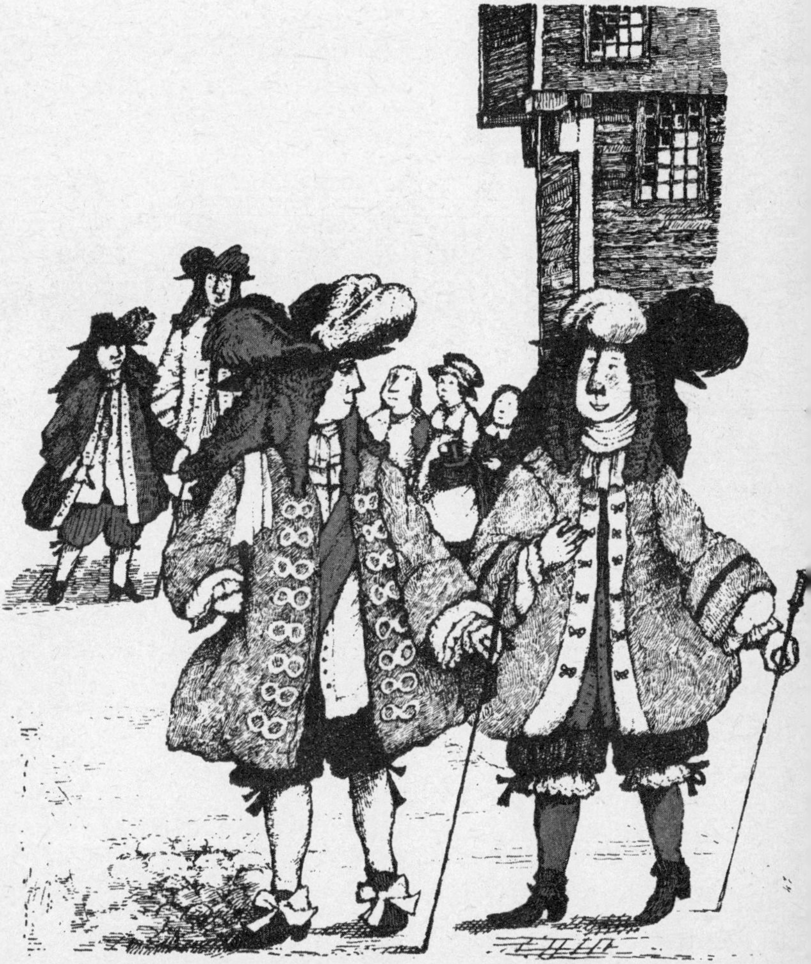

All Hartford went out to look at him
as he and his soldiers came trooping in.
It was growing late
when they came to town.
Sir Edmund was cross and hungry.
So he took his way
to a nearby inn,
at the sign of Ye Bunche of Grapes.

He called to the keeper of the inn.
"Master Zachariah Sanford!" called he.
"Bring us some beef
and some bread
and some beer.
And a hot rum toddy, at once, if you please.
At once, if you please,
and some beer."

Sir Edmund's men ate and drank
while the night grew dark and windy.

Then Sir Edmund called
the Connecticut men
to come and learn his wishes.
There were
Jonathan's father, Mr. Wadsworth,
and Roger's father, Mr. Wolcott,
and Mr. Stanly and Colonel Talcott,
and Andrew Leete,
and Governor Treat,
all the important Connecticut men,
and everyone else in Hartford, too.
They marched Sir Edmund Andros
into their sturdy meetinghouse
and sat him down
in Governor Treat's oaken chair.

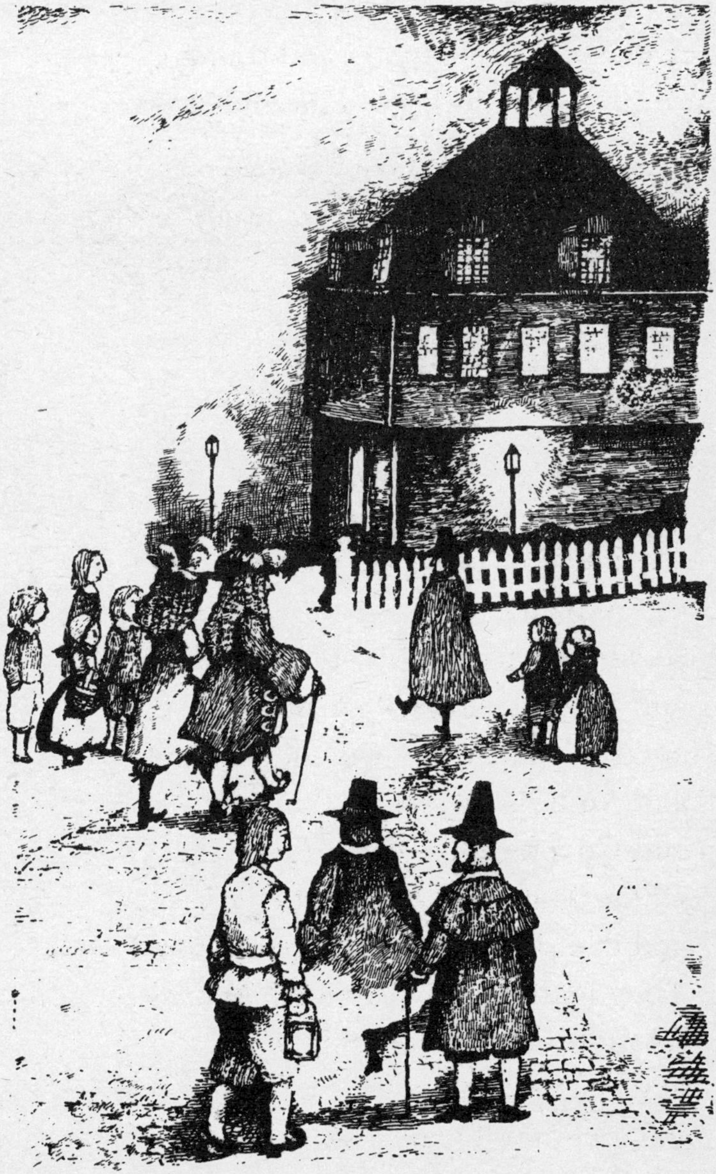

Young Jonathan Wadsworth
was in the crowd.
So were Roger and Hezekiah and Hannah.

And when the wind began to moan,
the children began to wonder
if Goody Gifford were out in the night
wailing about King Philip's head.
But the rest of the people of Hartford town
listened and watched
to see what Sir Edmund would say and do.
And Mr. Wadsworth and Mr. Wolcott
and Mr. Stanly and Colonel Talcott
and Andrew Leete and Governor Treat
argued and argued and argued.

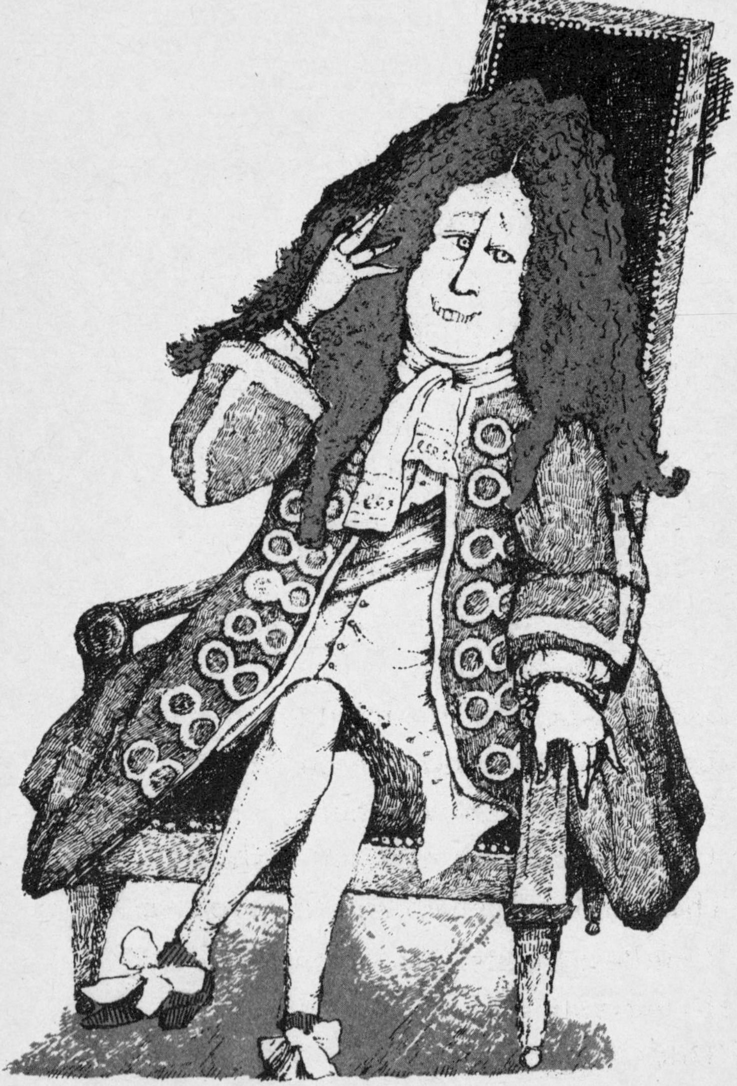

But Sir Edmund Andros
crossed his legs
and fluffed his wig
and shook his plume
and laughed and smiled and said:
"See here! Good King James
must have your charter back again."
So Mr. Wadsworth and Mr. Wolcott
and Mr. Stanly and Colonel Talcott
and Andrew Leete and Governor Treat
set the charter in plain sight,
and laid it by Sir Edmund's seat,
in the flickering candlelight.
"Odds fish! Me charter!"
Sir Edmund croaked,
and stretched out his hand for the paper.
But before he could take hold of it,
there came a rush of vapor!
A slam! A whoosh of wind! A shout!
The candles dimmed and flickered out!
"Candles! Lights!" Sir Edmund called.
He felt a stir and bustle.
"Odds fish! Me charter! Light the lights!"

He heard a paper rustle.
But when at last the lights came on,
Sir Edmund found the charter *gone!*

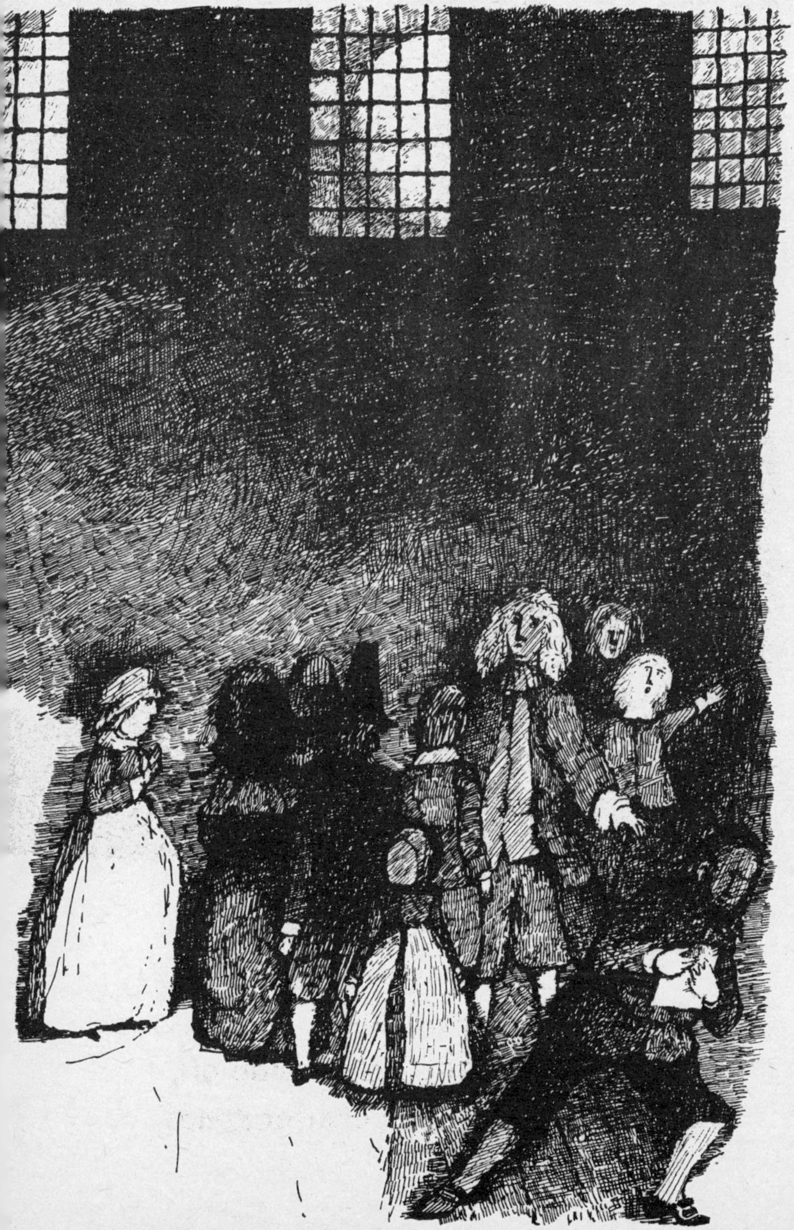

Chapter Five
THE CHARTER OAK

Not even young Jonathan Wadsworth
could learn
exactly what happened that Halloween—
even though he had been right there
in the meetinghouse
when all the lights went out.

When the candles were lit again,
he saw that Father was missing.

Everyone was talking at once.
Sir Edmund stamped his foot, in a rage.
But since nobody else noticed
that Father was gone,
Jonathan said nothing about it.

When Sir Edmund saw that the charter
was nowhere to be found,
he grew very calm and quiet.
Sir Edmund pretended
he wasn't the least bit angry
(though the tip of his nose grew red).
And Mr. Wolcott and Colonel Talcott
and Andrew Leete and Governor Treat
told him *they* knew nothing about it.
And at last they all went home to bed.

Next day Sir Edmund
marched out of Hartford,
taking his soldiers with him.
And so far as the people of Hartford cared,
that was the end of that.

Until many years later,
when King James
was no longer King of England,
long, long after
Sir Edmund Andros
had been sent home to London,
where he
belonged.
For then it was
that Mr. Wadsworth
brought the old charter
back to the Hartford meetinghouse.
He told everybody,
"Of course it was me!
I hid the charter
that Halloween.
I tucked it away
as safe as could be,
deep in the hollow
of the old oak tree!"

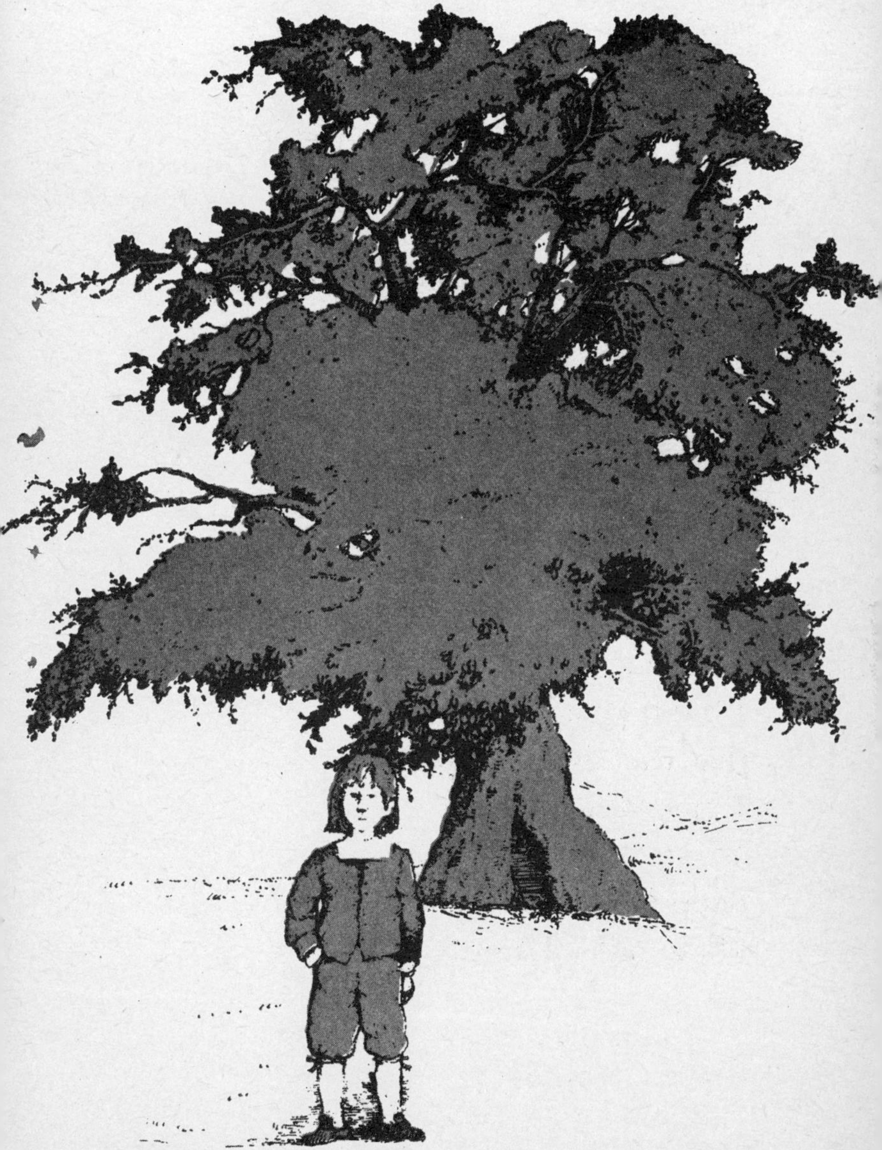

ABOUT THIS STORY

The story of how the Sachem's Tree, in Hartford, came to be named the Charter Oak, is one of Connecticut's oldest and dearest legends. Its most accurate historian of the colonial period, Benjamin Trumbull, said that on that night (October 31, 1687) "the charter was brought out and laid upon the table, where the assembly was sitting....The lights were instantly extinguished, and ... Capt. Wadsworth of Hartford, in the most silent and secret manner, carried off the charter and secreted it in a large hollow tree."

The colonial charter gave Connecticut a considerable amount of self-government. (Two copies, still sealed with traces of green sealing wax, are cherished to this day by Connecticut.) It was granted by King Charles II to John Winthrop, Jr., in 1662; and Charles' brother, James II, rescinded the privileges it granted (via his governor-general of the Dominion of New England, the officious Sir Edmund Andros) in

1687. For James II wished New Hampshire, Massa-
chusetts, Rhode Island, and Connecticut to be
welded into one single dominion—as indeed
they were for several years, until news of England's
"Glorious Revolution" of 1688 reached Boston in the
spring of 1689—at which time each of the four colonies again began governing itself separately.

(It may be interesting to remember, too, that when
Sir Edmund Andros came marching into Hartford in
1687, it was eleven years after New England's
severest Indian war—King Philip's War—had ended,
and that pirates such as Captain Kidd plagued the
New England coast and would continue to do so for
many years after this date, and that the Salem witch
trials would not take place for another five years. It
was a time of much lawlessness and superstition.)

There is absolutely no way of knowing whether or
not this legend of the hiding of the charter in the
Charter Oak is absolutely true. But it *is* certain that
Connecticut loved to tell the story and venerated the
old hollow tree until it fell, the victim of a thunder-
storm, on August 21, 1856. And since then, it has been
commemorated in paintings and in a postage stamp,
and it gave its name to the present bridge at Hartford
that spans the Connecticut River.

Even if the story is *not* true, there is no question
that Connecticut's jealousy of its rights and liberties
left its mark forever on our national Constitution and
on the egalitarian stamp of many of the laws of our
country. For that reason, I have retold the old story
here (adding a number of fanciful details of my own)
in a manner which, I hope, its ancient sons might not
entirely have disapproved.

About the Author

F. N. Monjo's historical easy-to-read books *Pirates in Panama*, *The One Bad Thing About Father*, *The Drinking Gourd* (an ALA Notable Book), and *Indian Summer* have received high acclaim, as have his books for older readers, *The Vicksburg Veteran* (an ALA Notable Book), *The Jezebel Wolf*, and *Slater's Mill*.

Mr. Monjo lives in New York City with his wife and four children.

About the Artist

Margot Tomes, a graduate of Pratt Institute, was born in Yonkers, New York.

She has illustrated several children's books, such as *Joe and the Talking Christmas Tree*, by Dale Fife; *Plenty for Three*, by Liesel Moak Skorpen; *A Secret House* and *Aaron and the Green Mountain Boys* (A Break-of-Day Book) by Patricia Lee Gauch. In addition to being a children's book illustrator, she is a textile designer.

Miss Tomes lives and works in New York City.